Melrose Public Library
DISCARDED

W9-BVT-036

TO AKITO
The Best Delivery Ever!

atheneum

ATHENEUM BOOKS FOR YOUNG READERS
An imprint of Simon & Schuster Children's Publishing Division
1230 Avenue of the Americas, New York, New York 10020
Copyright © 2017 by Aaron Meshon
All rights reserved, including the right of reproduction in whole or in part in any form.
ATHENEUM BOOKS FOR YOUNG READERS is a registered trademark of Simon & Schuster, Inc.
Atheneum logo is a trademark of Simon & Schuster, Inc.
For information about special discounts for bulk purchases, please contact Simon & Schuster
Special Sales at 1-866-506-1949 or business@simonandschuster.com.
The Simon & Schuster Speakers Bureau can bring authors to your live event. For more information
or to book an event, contact the Simon & Schuster Speakers Bureau at
1-866-248-3049 or visit our website at www.simonspeakers.com.
Book design by Ann Bobco
The text for this book was hand-lettered.
The illustrations for this book were digitally rendered.

Manufactured in China
1016 SCP
First Edition
10 9 8 7 6 5 4 3 2 1
Library of Congress Cataloging-in-Publication Data
Names: Meshon, Aaron, author, illustrator.
Title: Delivery / by Aaron Meshon.
Description: First edition. | New York : Atheneum Books for Young Readers, [2017] | Summary:
In this nearly wordless picture book, a grandmother uses every creative means of transportation
necessary to deliver cookies to her grandson on his birthday.
Identifiers: LCCN 2015024924 | ISBN 9781481441759 (hardcover) | ISBN 9781481441766
(eBook)
Subjects: | CYAC: Grandmothers—Fiction. | Transportation—Fiction. | Birthdays—Fiction.
Classification: LCC PZ7.M5492 De 2017 | DDC [E]—dc23
LC record available at http://lccn.loc.gov/2015024924

DELI♥ERY

BY AARON MESHON

'CHILDRENS ROOM
MELROSE PUBLIC LIBRARY

Atheneum Books for Young Readers * New York London Toronto Sydney New Delhi

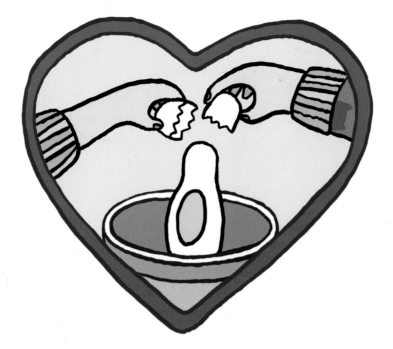

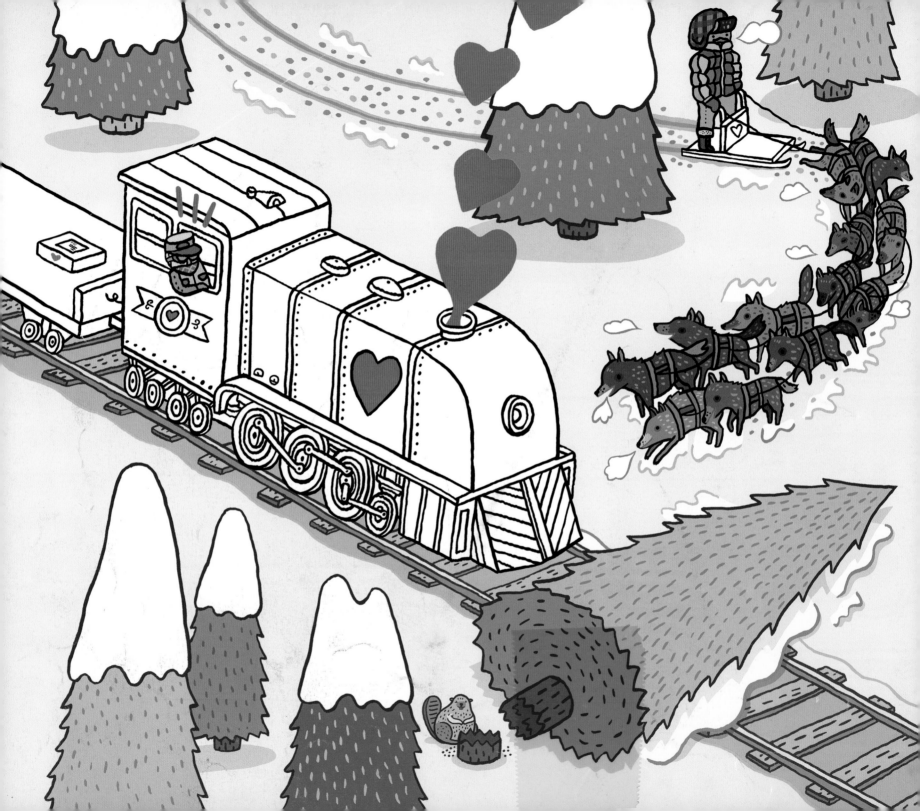